HE WHO GETS SLAPPED

and other plays

by LEONID ANDREYEV

adapted by WALTER WYKES

D1520622

Black Box Press
Los Angeles

P6
3452
A2
2007

CONTENTS

HE WHO GETS SLAPPED

by LEONID ANDREYEV

adapted by WALTER WYKES

CHARACTERS:

PAULIE, *a clown*
WALLY, *a clown*
PAPA BRIQUET, *manager of the circus*
COUNT MANCINI, *an aristocrat*
XENA, *a lion tamer*
HE, *a clown*
JACKSON, *a clown*
CONSUELO, *a bareback rider*
BEZANO, *a bareback rider*
BARON REGNARD, *an aristocrat*
A GENTLEMAN
USHER #1
USHER #2
USHER #3
OTHER PERFORMERS

ACT I

*[A circus. Backstage. Posters everywhere. Enter
PAULIE and WALLY, two clowns marching and
playing kazoos.]*

PAULIE: Stop!

WALLY: What?

PAULIE: You're off!

WALLY: *I'm* off?

PAULIE: Yes!

WALLY: I'm not off! You're off!

PAULIE: *I'm* off?!

WALLY: That's right.

PAULIE: How can I be off—it's my song!

WALLY: But you keep changing it!

PAULIE: No!

WALLY: Yes!

PAULIE: No! Listen!
*[He stands close to WALLY and plays into his face.
When he is finished, WALLY shrugs.]*

WALLY: From the top?

PAULIE: From the top!
*[As the clowns resume their march, PAPA BRIQUET
storms toward them. The ringmaster and manager of
the circus, he is red in the face.]*

PAPA BRIQUET: You make me sick!
[The clowns freeze, astonished.]

WALLY: What did *we* do?

PAULIE: We're just rehearsing.

WALLY: March of the ants.

PAPA BRIQUET: Not you! Him!
> *[Enter COUNT MANCINI. He carries himself with an aristocratic air, and, when he laughs, his thin sharp face takes on a marked resemblance to a satyr.]*

MANCINI: I beg your pardon?
> *[PAULIE and WALLY quietly retreat.]*

PAPA BRIQUET: You heard me! You stick your nose where it doesn't belong and provoke the artists while they're trying to work! Someday you'll get a beating, and I promise you, I won't interfere!

MANCINI: You can't really expect a man of my station to treat the performers as equals. I speak with *you* quite familiarly—what more do you expect?

PAPA BRIQUET: Now you're really asking for it!

MANCINI: And if they did attack me—
> *[He produces a derringer from the handle of his cane and aims it at PAPA BRIQUET.]*
Useful little thing.

PAPA BRIQUET: Put that gun away.

MANCINI: By the way, you wouldn't believe the little treasure I dug up on the subway yesterday. What a beauty! Eyes like sunshine and legs that—
> *[He laughs.]*
Well, I know you don't approve of such sport. Look, give me a hundred dollars, and I'll relieve you of my unpleasant company.

PAPA BRIQUET: Not a dime.

MANCINI: All right, Briquet. You leave me no choice. I'll have to take Consuelo.

PAPA BRIQUET: Your daily threat!

MANCINI: What would you do in my position? You know I have to keep up appearances. Family reputation and all that. Is it my fault I've had a run of bad luck that's forced me to make my daughter a bareback rider in your silly circus? We can't be allowed to starve! Fifty dollars.

PAPA BRIQUET: I won't contribute to your depravities.

MANCINI: My depravities?

PAPA BRIQUET: You're a predator! You chase young girls half your age!

MANCINI: They know what they're doing.

PAPA BRIQUET: They don't have any choice! They're desperate for their next meal!

MANCINI: Which I'm happy to provide.

PAPA BRIQUET: You prey on their unfortunate circumstances! And just because they consent to your perverted little games doesn't mean you're free and clear! Mark my words, Mancini—you'll end up in jail one of these days!

MANCINI: Jail? Don't be ridiculous! I have to uphold the family name— don't I? The Mancinis are known for their love of young girls! It's a family tradition! Is it my fault I have to pay for what my ancestors got free of charge? I don't drink, I stopped playing cards after that unfortunate incident with the police—there's no reason to laugh—now if I give up girls, what will be left of Mancini?! A coat of arms?! Fifty dollars, and I'm on my way.

PAPA BRIQUET: I told you no.
            [Enter XENA, a lion tamer.]

MANCINI: Madame Xena!
            [He takes her hand and kneels.]
This barbarian may murder me in my sleep, but I cannot suppress my feelings for you one moment longer! You are a goddess! A queen among women! Come away with me! Leave this brute to his clowns and his jugglers! He can never appreciate your radiant beauty!

XENA: And you can?

MANCINI: I am an expert in such matters.

XENA: *[To PAPA BRIQUET.]* Money?

PAPA BRIQUET: Yes.

XENA: Don't give him any.

MANCINI: Ah! Such cruelty from one so beautiful—it isn't natural. I'm not one of your beasts to be whipped before the crowd!

XENA: Jackson tells me you've hired a tutor for Consuelo. What for?

MANCINI: What for?! She's the daughter of a Count! Shouldn't she have the finest education?

PAPA BRIQUET: If I were the government, I'd forbid all artists to read books. It ruins them.

XENA: I like a good book every now and then.

PAPA BRIQUET: I'm not talking about the kind of books you read.

MANCINI: You surprise me, Briquet. Are you really an enemy of enlightenment?

PAPA BRIQUET: Why not? What has education ever done for anybody? It just makes them restless!

MANCINI: How do you expect improvement without education?

PAPA BRIQUET: I don't expect anything. You're an educated man, Mancini. You've read all the important books. What has it taught you— how to strip young girls of their dignity? How to live like a parasite off your own daughter?

MANCINI: I resent that remark. I would do anything for Consuelo. In fact, I have a little something in the works right now.

XENA: The Baron, you mean?

PAPA BRIQUET: Don't get any ideas. Remember—I have her under contract.

MANCINI: Such base formalities.

XENA: Give him ten dollars and make him go away.

MANCINI: Ten! Never! Twenty at least! I simply can't do with any less—even the dirtiest street urchin costs that much.

XENA: Disgusting.

PAPA BRIQUET: *[Gives MANCINI a twenty dollar bill.]* Here. Get out of my sight.

MANCINI: Much obliged.
                          [Enter PAULIE and WALLY.]

PAULIE: Papa Briquet—

WALLY: —there's someone here to see you.

PAULIE: I think he's drunk.

WALLY: Drunk or crazy.

PAPA BRIQUET: What does he want?

PAULIE: *[Shrugs.]* Didn't say.

WALLY: But he looks important.

PAULIE: Looks loaded.

PAPA BRIQUET: Loaded as in booze—or money?

PAULIE: Both.

WALLY: And a little crazy to boot.

PAPA BRIQUET: Send him back.
                          *[PAULIE and WALLY exit. PAPA BRIQUET turns to
                          MANCINI.]*
Why are you still here?

MANCINI: I want to see your mysterious guest.

XENA: The red lion's nervous today.

PAPA BRIQUET: What?

XENA: The red lion. He's restless.

PAPA BRIQUET: What do you want me to do?

XENA: I'm just telling you.

PAPA BRIQUET: I don't like that damn animal. He's too unpredictable.

XENA: Do you want me to cut him?

PAPA BRIQUET: No. He's the best part of your act.
          *[Enter a STRANGER in formal attire, escorted by the
          two clowns.]*

STRANGER: Excuse me … are you the manager?

PAPA BRIQUET: Papa Briquet. What can I do for you?

STRANGER: *[Indicating XENA and MANCINI.]* And these are your artists?

MANCINI: *[Laughs.]* No, no! I'm Count Mancini.

STRANGER: Count?

MANCINI: That's right. And who might you be?

STRANGER: Well … I'm not really sure yet. I mean, I haven't chosen a
name. I thought you might offer some advice. I have a few ideas, but they
don't have the right ring—too literary, you know.

PAPA BRIQUET: Too literary?

STRANGER: Yes. Too sophisticated. I'm looking for something … I don't
know … a little more straightforward.
          [Indicating PAULIE and WALLY.]
Are these your clowns?

PAPA BRIQUET: That would seem obvious.

STRANGER: *[To PAULIE and WALLY.]* And what are your names?

PAULIE: I'm Paulie.

WALLY: And I'm Wally.

STRANGER: *[Smiles.]* They rhyme! Your names, I mean.

XENA: He's a quick one.

PAPA BRIQUET: What exactly can I do for you? Are you looking to rent the place out? A special engagement maybe?

STRANGER: Oh, no—it's not what you can do for me, but what I can do for you!

PAPA BRIQUET: And what can you do for me?

STRANGER: I want to be one of your performers!

PAPA BRIQUET: One of my performers?

STRANGER: Yes!

PAPA BRIQUET: Are you drunk?

STRANGER: I don't drink.

PAULIE: Not at all?

WALLY: Not even a little bit?

STRANGER: No.

PAPA BRIQUET: Are you crazy?

STRANGER: *[Laughs.]* Perhaps. Nevertheless, I would like to be a performer.

PAPA BRIQUET: Do you have any experience?

STRANGER: What do you mean?

PAPA BRIQUET: Experience. In the circus.

STRANGER: Well …

MANCINI: You look like a society man.

STRANGER: Unfortunately, yes. But I'd like to be a clown.

MANCINI: *[Laughs.]* A clown!

PAULIE: What's so funny?

WALLY: Yeah—what's wrong with being a clown?!

MANCINI: He's joking! He's obviously pulling your leg! Is there a hidden camera?

STRANGER: This is no joke. I'm very serious.

PAPA BRIQUET: But what can you do? Do you have any skills?

STRANGER: *[Laughs.]* No! None! Isn't that funny! I can't do anything!

WALLY: That is funny.

PAULIE: He's got something there.

PAPA BRIQUET: I'm afraid all our positions are filled.

STRANGER: There must be something I could do! We can invent something! Maybe a nice little speech on politics or religion! Something like a … a debate among clowns!

WALLY: Is he joking?

MANCINI: Sounds hilarious.

PAPA BRIQUET: Get Jackson.

PAULIE AND WALLY: Jackson! Jackson!
                    [Enter JACKSON, another clown.]

PAPA BRIQUET: This is Jackson. Our most famous clown.

STRANGER: *[Shaking JACKSON'S hand.]* Oh! It's a pleasure to finally meet you! Really! You're a genius! A real genius!

JACKSON: I like him.

STRANGER: I've watched you perform! So many nights!

PAPA BRIQUET: He wants to be a clown.

JACKSON: A clown?

STRANGER: Yes!

PAPA BRIQUET: What do you think?

JACKSON: Well, let me take a look.
> *[The STRANGER excitedly removes his coat and prepares for the examination.]*
Hmmm … turn around. That's it. Now smile. Wider. Broader. Do you call that a smile? Big! That's more like it. I don't suppose you can do a cartwheel.

STRANGER: *[Sighs.]* No.

JACKSON: Somersault?

STRANGER: I'm afraid not.

JACKSON: How old are you?

STRANGER: Thirty-nine. Too late?
> *[JACKSON moves away with a whistle. Silence.]*

XENA: Take him.

PAPA BRIQUET: What?! What the hell do you think I'm going to do with him?! He can't even do a somersault! Besides, he's drunk!

STRANGER: Honestly, I'm not.
> *[Enter CONSUELO and BEZANO, two bareback riders.]*

CONSUELO: Daddy!
[She kisses MANCINI on the cheek.]
Are you staying for the show?

MANCINI: No, not tonight—I've been watching the show backstage.
[To the STRANGER.]
This is my daughter, Countess Veronica. But her stage name is—

STRANGER: Consuelo! Yes, I know! I've enjoyed her work! It's marvelous! Really amazing!

CONSUELO: There's nothing to it, really.

MANCINI: Oh, don't be so modest. She is remarkable. Everyone says so. In fact, don't you think she's due for a raise, Briquet?

PAPA BRIQUET: Don't start.

STRANGER: Everyone here is so interesting! I really would like to stay! There must be something I could do … something unique … something that doesn't require any real talent …
[He thinks.]
I've got it!

WALLY: He's got it!

STRANGER: I shall be he who gets slapped!
[General laughter.]
You see! I made you laugh!

JACKSON: "He Who Gets Slapped." That's not bad.

XENA: I like it. Straightforward. Not too literary.
[JACKSON suddenly steps forward and gives a circus slap to the STRANGER who is somewhat startled.]

HE: *[Rubbing his cheek.]* What was that?

JACKSON: He Who Gets Slapped. That's the bit, right?
[The others laugh.]

HE: How funny … it didn't really hurt at all … although my cheek burns a little.

WALLY: He says he'd like another.
> *[JACKSON gives HE another slap. More laughter.*
> *This time, HE laughs along with the others.]*

JACKSON: *[To PAPA BRIQUET.]* Take him. I think we can do something with him after all.

PAPA BRIQUET: All right, but he's your responsibility.

WALLY: Congratulations!

PAULIE: Welcome to the circus!
> *[WALLY and PAULIE march around HE, playing their*
> *kazoos.]*

HE: Thank you! Thank you!

JACKSON: Do you like music? I can teach you how to play a Beethoven sonata on a broom, or Mozart on a bottle?

HE: I'm not very good with music, but I'd love to learn. A clown! My childhood dream! When all my friends were thinking of sports and literature and science—I dreamed of clowns. Beethoven on a broom! Mozart on a bottle! This is what I've wanted all my life! Oh! I need a costume!

JACKSON: Yes, a costume must be chosen very carefully. Have you seen my Sun here?
> *[He displays a sun emblazoned on his posterior.]*
It took me two years to come up with this.

HE: It's wonderful. I'll start thinking right away.

MANCINI: Well, this has been thoroughly entertaining, but I'm afraid I have a pressing engagement that I simply cannot miss. Goodbye.
> *[MANCINI exits, followed by PAULIE and WALLY*
> *playing a funeral march on their kazoos. HE and*
> *JACKSON laugh.]*

BEZANO: *[To CONSUELO.]* We'd better get back to work.

CONSUELO: All right.
                [To HE.]
Congratulations.
                [Exit BEZANO and CONSUELO.]

JACKSON: Give that costume some thought, HE. I'll think it over, too. Be here at ten o'clock tomorrow morning. And don't be late, or you'll get another slap!
                [He laughs. Exit JACKSON.]

PAPA BRIQUET: Well, I suppose we should talk money then.

HE: Oh, you don't have to pay me. I've got enough money.

PAPA BRIQUET: He does have potential!
                [To XENA.]
Draw up the contract! Get that in writing!

XENA: *[Producing an official-looking book.]* We have to put down the names of all our performers, you know—government regulations. Just in case of an accident. So … what's yours?

HE: *[Smiling.]* HE. I just chose it—didn't you hear?

XENA: No, your real name. Do you have a passport?

HE: A passport? No. I mean, yes, but … I had no idea the rules would be strictly enforced here. What do you need my name for?
                [XENA and PAPA BRIQUET exchange a glance.]

PAPA BRIQUET: Is there some reason you don't want to give us your name?

HE: Yes. There is.

PAPA BRIQUET: Then we can't take you. I'm sorry.

XENA: We don't want any trouble with the police.

PAPA BRIQUET: You might get hurt or kill yourself doing something stupid. Personally, I don't care. A corpse is just a corpse. It's up to God and the Devil to sort out. But the police—they're curious. They want names.

HE: I … I thought here, of all places, I could lose my past.

PAPA BRIQUET: Something to hide, eh?

HE: Can't you just pretend I have no name? That I've lost it—like I might lose my hat or a shoe? Or let someone else take it by mistake? When a stray dog shows up at the door, you don't ask his name—you just give him another. Let me be that dog.
                    [Laughs.]
HE—the dog!

XENA: Why don't you just tell us your name—just the two of us. Nobody else needs to know.

PAPA BRIQUET: Unless you happen to break your neck.
                    [HE hesitates.]

XENA: Whatever your secret—it's safe with us.
                    [Pause.]

HE: All right.
                    [HE produces a passport. XENA takes it and looks it over. Surprised, she passes it on to PAPA BRIQUET.]

PAPA BRIQUET: Is this really true? Are you really—

HE: Please … this person no longer exists. It's just a name—a check for an old hat. Forget it, as I have. I am He Who Gets Slapped—nothing more.
                    [Pause.]

PAPA BRIQUET: Are you sure you're not drunk?

XENA: It's his business. Leave him alone.

PAPA BRIQUET: *[Shrugs.]* You're a strange man, HE. But who am I to question? All right, come on. I'll show you the dressing room.

HE: Thank you. I'm so happy. I really feel like I belong here. But it still seems like a dream. I won't believe it until I feel the sawdust under my feet—until I stand in the ring where I will get my slaps!

XENA: Send Bezano in, will you? I need to settle an account with him.

[HE and PAPA BRIQUET exit. XENA studies her book.
After a moment, BEZANO appears in the doorway.]
BEZANO: You wanted to see me?

XENA: Sit.

BEZANO: I'm in the middle of a rehearsal.

XENA: With Consuelo?

BEZANO: Yeah.

XENA: Do you love her?

BEZANO: What?

XENA: Are you in love with the little witch?
                    [Pause.]

BEZANO: No.

XENA: No?

BEZANO: I don't love anybody. How can I? Who am I? An acrobat. A bareback rider. She's the daughter of a count. He could take her away tomorrow.

XENA: He will, you know. One of these days.

BEZANO: I know.

XENA: He's trying to marry her off to a rich baron.

BEZANO: Have you seen the man? He's a pig.

XENA: And what about me? Do you love me, Bezano?

BEZANO: No. I told you before.

XENA: Still no? Not even a little?

BEZANO: *[Pauses.]* How could I love you? I'm afraid of you.

XENA: Am I really so terrifying? Am I such a monster?

BEZANO: You're beautiful. Almost as beautiful as Consuelo.

XENA: Almost?

BEZANO: But I don't like your eyes. They command me to love you—and I don't like to take orders.

XENA: Do I command? Or do I only implore?

BEZANO: You look at me like you look at your lions.

XENA: My red lion loves me—

BEZANO: If he loves you, why is he so restless?

XENA: Yesterday, he licked my hand like a dog.

BEZANO: Do you want me to lick your hand too—like a dog?

XENA: No. I want to lick your hand. Give it to me.
          [She takes BEZANO'S hand—tries to put it in her mouth.]

BEZANO: Stop!
          [HE appears in the doorway.]

XENA: Why do you torture me like this, Bezano? You know I love you.

BEZANO: Let go of me! Stop it! Let go!
          [As BEZANO pulls away, they become aware of HE standing in the doorway. There is an awkward pause. BEZANO rushes out of the room. Silence.]

HE: I'm sorry. I … I forgot my coat.
          [Pause.]
I didn't hear anything.

XENA: I don't care what you heard.

HE: I … I thought you and Papa Briquet—

XENA: It's none of your business.
                    [HE turns to go.]
Look at me, HE. Look at my body. My legs. My face. My breasts. Now,
tell me—what do you think of a man who would turn all this down?

HE: I … I really don't know.

XENA: Is he really a man, or just a stupid beast?

HE: I'm not sure I understand.

XENA: Oh, HE … what can I do to make my lions love me?

* * *

ACT II

[CONSUELO and BARON REGNARD sit backstage. She wears her stage costume. He wears a tuxedo. The sound of the evening performance can be heard in the background—laughter, shrieks, music, and applause.]

CONSUELO: It was nice of you to come tonight, Baron.

BARON: I didn't have much choice. Your father made it very clear that if I didn't come he would transfer the invitation to a certain Marquis Justi.

CONSUELO: Oh, he's only trying to make you jealous. I've heard him speak of the Marquis, but I've never even seen him.

BARON: He's a very rich man. And you father is very clever.

CONSUELO: Why do you say that?
[Pause.]

BARON: Did you like the jewels I sent?

CONSUELO: They were beautiful.

BARON: Then why did you return them?

CONSUELO: Father made me. I didn't want to. I even cried a little.

BARON: It was clever of him to return them. He's positioning himself for a bigger prize.

CONSUELO: But they were so beautiful—your jewels.

BARON: Not as beautiful as you, Consuelo.

CONSUELO: You're going to make me blush.

BARON: Everyone is in love with you, you know. They all want to kiss that pretty little mouth of yours.

CONSUELO: Do you want to kiss my pretty little mouth, Baron?

BARON: I'd like to do more than that.

CONSUELO: Well ... talk it over with father.

BARON: Your father won't be satisfied unless I marry you. And I can't do that.

CONSUELO: Why not? Isn't that what this is all about?

BARON: Don't be absurd. I couldn't possibly.

CONSUELO: Then why are you here?

BARON: I love you, Consuelo!

CONSUELO: But you just said—

BARON: I can't marry you, but I still want you!

CONSUELO: Are you suggesting—

BARON: Yes!

CONSUELO: I'm not your plaything, Baron—a toy to do with as you please.

BARON: And if I were that other acrobat—what's his name? Bezano? Would you refuse me then?

CONSUELO: Bezano's all right, but he's more interested in his horses than he is in me. Still, HE says that Bezano and I are the most beautiful couple in the world. HE calls us Adam and Eve.

BARON: Who is this HE?

CONSUELO: The new clown.

BARON: Ahh, yes.

CONSUELO: He's so funny! He got fifty-two slaps yesterday! We counted them. Imagine, fifty-two slaps!

BARON: I don't like him. I've seen the way he looks at you.

CONSUELO: Oh, don't be ridiculous. HE only likes to talk. Half the time I don't know what he's talking about. It's almost as if he was drunk.

BARON: I'm drunk! With love!

CONSUELO: But if you won't marry—

BARON: What if I shoot myself? Would you believe I love you then?

CONSUELO: Only if you leave a tragic note behind proclaiming your eternal devotion and calling me all kinds of pretty names.

BARON: Consuelo, you little minx, it's unbearable! I've had hundreds of women—beautiful women, every which way! But I never saw them! You are the first woman I have ever seen! Let me kiss you!

CONSUELO: No.
            [The BARON grabs her roughly.]

BARON: Consuelo—

CONSUELO: Don't. Get up. Let go of my hand!

BARON: Consuelo!

CONSUELO: Get up! It's disgusting! You're so fat!
            *[The BARON pulls away from her, his face red. Voices
            are heard approaching. The clowns enter, talking
            excitedly. HE leads them in his new costume and
            painted face.]*

WALLY: A hundred slaps!

PAULIE: Bravo, HE!

JACKSON: Not bad! Not bad at all!

WALLY: He was the professor today, and we were the students. Here goes another!
            *[WALLY gives HE a clown's slap. HE feigns surprise.
            Laughter. Everyone pats HE on the back. BEZANO
            rushes in, looking around anxiously.]*

BEZANO: Consuelo! We're on!
> *[CONSUELO rushes out with BEZANO. MANCINI enters and makes his way towards the BARON.]*

MANCINI: What a success! How the crowd loves slaps!
> *[Whispering.]*

Your knees are dusty, Baron. Brush them off. The floor is dirty in here.
> *[The BARON dusts himself off and exits.]*

JACKSON: I'm an old clown, HE, and I know the crowd. But today, you have eclipsed me—the clouds have covered my Sun.
> *[He strikes the Sun on his posterior.]*

HE: But why didn't you let me finish my speech? I was just getting started.

JACKSON: The crowd doesn't want speeches! They want slaps! Believe me, I cut you off just in time!

PAPA BRIQUET: He's right. This isn't a church or a debate hall. It's a circus. You forget yourself, HE.

HE: But they loved me!

PAPA BRIQUET: You were lucky. Your performance was sloppy. A good slap must be clean—right side, left side, and done with it. They will laugh and love you. Don't muddy the effect with cheap theatrics—politics, religion, that sort of nonsense.
> *[A buzzer sounds.]*

To the ring! To the ring!
> *[The clowns rush back to the stage. PAPA BRIQUET stops HE.]*

Not you, HE. Take a break.
> *[PAPA BRIQUET exits. Silence. MANCINI produces a flask of whiskey and drinks.]*

HE: Drinking tonight, Count?

MANCINI: Might as well.

HE: Trouble with one of your girls?

MANCINI: How did you know?

HE: Just a guess.

MANCINI: You should see her. Little temptress. Black hair. Eyes as dark as night. And her smile! So ... bewitching! Like the devil's bride! Like Eve, holding the apple! Her eyes sparkling! Just daring you! Laughing! Begging you to take a bite! Promising untold pleasures if you just have the courage to grasp it—to take her in your arms! How can a man be expected to resist such temptation?!
[Pause.]
You're the only one who understands me, HE. Why don't I like things which aren't forbidden? Why should I always, even at the moment of ecstasy, be reminded of some stupid law?! This passion, I'm telling you, it'll turn my hair gray and lead me to the grave—or prison.
[Pause.]
Is it really my fault if she's a few years younger than the law allows? I mean, how was I to know? Eh? Besides, it's only our society, you know, that makes it such a crime. In the old days, it was quite normal. It was expected. Everybody did it. Mary and Joseph even. She was only thirteen, you know. Nobody judges *them*. And you can't tell me she didn't know exactly what she was doing! This girl—not the virgin mother. I didn't teach her anything, if you know what I mean. But her parents don't see it that way. And they know they've got me by the throat.
[Pause.]
I can't go to jail, HE. I wouldn't last a month. I'm an intellectual—a man of refinement. The jails in this country ... they don't discriminate between men of my kind and real criminals. They'd eat me alive.

HE: Isn't there any way of settling the matter out of court?

MANCINI: Sure. Money. They want money. Which I haven't got.

HE: And the Baron won't help you?

MANCINI: The Baron knows all about my predicament! He knows he'll get what he's after, so he's looking for a bargain. Trying to drive down the price. But what can I do? I've got my head in the noose. Sooner or later, I'll be forced to give him Consuelo for a song. Twenty thousand. Maybe ten.

HE: That's quite a bargain. For him, I mean.

MANCINI: Did I say it was anything else? I don't want to do it. But if this girl's family doesn't drop the charges soon, I'll spend a good number of years in a prison cell, and I'm fairly certain I won't find anything to my liking there!

HE: Give Consuelo to the acrobat.

MANCINI: Bezano? Are you joking? He doesn't have any money. And besides, he doesn't care for her any more than the Baron does.

HE: Then give her to me.

MANCINI: To you?!
                    [Laughs.]
Do you have some hidden fortune? Some magic lamp that can erase my troubles?

HE: I'm not joking.
                    [Pause.]

MANCINI: I'll never get used to those faces. I don't care what they say, clowns aren't funny—they're scary as all hell!

HE: He won't marry her. Play it however you like. He's only looking for a little fun.

MANCINI: He'll marry her, all right. As long as she doesn't give him the milk for free.

HE: Consuelo isn't educated. Any decent housemaid has better manners.

MANCINI: What use does a woman have for education? Put her in a pretty dress and what does it matter? Consuelo is an unpolished jewel, and only a real ass doesn't notice her sparkle. Do you know what happened? I tried to polish her—

HE: Yes, you hired a tutor. What happened?

MANCINI: I got frightened. It was going too fast. Another month or two and she would have realized she didn't need me at all. So I dismissed him.
                    [Laughs.]
The clever old diamond merchants keep their precious stones unpolished to fool the thieves. My father taught me that.

HE: The sleep of a diamond. So … she's only sleeping then.
>   *[Pause.]*
You're wiser than I thought, Count.

MANCINI: Do you know what blood flows through the veins of an Italian
woman? The blood of Hannibal and Corsini! Of a Borgia—and of a dirty
Lombardi peasant! All possibilities, all forms are included in her, as in our
national sculpture! Do you understand? Strike here—and out springs a
washerwoman or a cheap street whore. Strike there—but carefully and
gently, and out springs a queen, a goddess, the Venus of the Capitol, who
sings like a Stradivarius and makes you cry with her beauty! An Italian
woman—

HE: But what kind will the Baron make of her?

MANCINI: What kind? A baroness! What else?
>   *[HE laughs.]*
Why are you laughing? I don't understand you.
>   *[Listening.]*
Why is it so quiet out there?

HE: Out there, it may be quiet. But in here—
>   *[HE taps MANCINI'S forehead.]*
—a whirlwind!
>   *[An USHER enters with a letter.]*

USHER #1: Excuse me … Count Mancini? The Baron asked me to give
you this letter.

MANCINI: *[Taking the letter.]* The Baron? Where is he?

USHER #1: He left.

MANCINI: Left?
>   *[The USHER nods.]*
The devil take him! And his money!
>   *[As MANCINI tears open the letter, the USHER turns to
>   go.]*

HE: Wait. Why is there no music? What's going on out there?

USHER #1: It's the act with Madame Xena and her lions.

[The USHER goes. MANCINI reads the BARON'S note for a second time.]

MANCINI: I can't believe it!

HE: What?

MANCINI: It's decided! He's going to marry her! He's going to marry Consuelo! My prayers have been answered! Congratulate me, HE! The Baron has swooped in with his fortune, and I'm saved!
[PAPA BRIQUET stumbles in, his face ashen.]

PAPA BRIQUET: Oh!

HE: Papa Briquet?

PAPA BRIQUET: Oh!

HE: What's wrong?

PAPA BRIQUET: I ... I can't ...

MANCINI: Has something happened? Has there been some sort of accident?

PAPA BRIQUET: I can't watch! She's insane! I think she really is! I can't watch! They'll tear her to pieces! Her lions—

MANCINI: Oh, come on, Briquet. She's always like that. What's wrong with you?

PAPA BRIQUET: No! Today she's really mad! She gone over the edge! Something's snapped. The crowd—they watch like dead people. They're not even breathing. Listen.
[They listen. Silence.]

HE: *[Disturbed.]* I'll go and see.

PAPA BRIQUET: No! I don't want to know! The red lion—you should see his eyes! It's terrible!

HE: Get him something to drink.

PAPA BRIQUET: I don't want anything! Oh, if only it were over!
[Suddenly the silence breaks, like a huge stone wall crashing—shouts, wild screams—half bestial, half human—mixed with music and applause. The men sigh, relieved.]

MANCINI: There! You see! I told you it was nothing, you old fool.
[Enter XENA, alone. She looks like a madwoman, or a drunken bacchante. Her hair falls over her shoulders, disheveled. She walks unseeing, though her eyes are afire. Behind her, the other performers slowly appear, pale and silent. They watch XENA, afraid to speak—as if the slightest sound might snap her sanity.]

PAPA BRIQUET: You're crazy! You're a madwoman!

XENA: *[Smiles, drunken with victory.]* Did you see? Did you?! They do love me!

JACKSON: Get her a chair.
[BEZANO fetches a chair. XENA sits.]

XENA: Did you see, Bezano? My lions love me!
[BEZANO exits without answering.]

WALLY: *[To XENA.]* Do you want some music?
[He plays his kazoo.]

PAPA BRIQUET: Get away from her! She doesn't need music—she needs to go home! She needs a doctor! Come on, I'll take you.

PAULIE: You can't go, Papa—there's still your number.

PAPA BRIQUET: To hell with my number.

CONSUELO: She … she didn't feed them today.

PAPA BRIQUET: What?

CONSUELO: She didn't feed them. The lions. I told her it was dangerous, but—

XENA: I wanted them ravenous. I wanted to test them. And I did!

PAPA BRIQUET: You are insane! They're wild animals! They could have eaten you alive!

XENA: They love me—didn't you see?

PAPA BRIQUET: Talk to her, HE. You're a man of the world. Maybe she'll listen to you.

HE: I … I don't—

PAPA BRIQUET: Explain it to her! Who is it possible for those hairy beasts to love?!

HE: Well … their own kind, I should think.

PAPA BRIQUET: Exactly! Their own kind! There! Do you hear!

JACKSON: Take it easy, Briquet. She isn't herself tonight.
             [XENA rises, trembling now, but still maintaining her queen-like composure.]

XENA: Take me home.

PAPA BRIQUET: Fine. Let's go.

XENA: Not you. Finish the show. Mancini will take me.

PAPA BRIQUET: Mancini?

MANCINI: Of course. I would be honored, Madame Xena.
             [To PAPA BRIQUET.]
Have no fear Briquet, I shall conduct her safely home.
             [MANCINI guides XENA toward the door. The other performers drift slowly back to the ring. PAPA BRIQUET is the last to go, leaving only HE and CONSUELO. From the ring, music, shrieks, and laughter are again audible.]

CONSUELO: It's so sad.

HE: Why did she do it?

CONSUELO: Because she isn't happy.

HE: But to take such a chance—

CONSUELO: If one isn't happy … maybe it's the best thing.

HE: Do you really believe that?

CONSUELO: I don't know. Maybe.
                    [Pause.]

HE: She's in love with Bezano?

CONSUELO: Bezano? My Bezano?

HE: Yes.

CONSUELO: But she's so old.
                    [HE Laughs.]
I like your costume, HE. Did you come up with it yourself?

HE: Jackson helped.

CONSUELO: Jackson is nice. All clowns are nice.

HE: I am wicked.

CONSUELO: *[Laughs.]* You? You're the nicest of them all!

HE: On the outside. But on the inside …
                    [HE makes a scary face. She laughs.]

CONSUELO: Are you going to watch me perform tonight?

HE: I always do.

CONSUELO: I can see you. In the wings.

HE: You're so beautiful.

CONSUELO: *[Smiles.]* Little Eve?

HE: Yes. But is Little Eve happy?

CONSUELO: Sure.

HE: What if the Baron asks you to marry him—will you?

CONSUELO: Of course. I don't love him. But I'll be his honest, faithful wife. What else am I going to do—work in the circus all my life?

HE: Are those your words—"his honest, faithful wife"?
        [Pause.]

CONSUELO: Who painted the laughter on your face?

HE: This? I did it myself.

CONSUELO: How do you do it—all of you? I tried once, but it was awful.

HE: I could teach you.

CONSUELO: That would be nice. Why are there no women clowns? Why is that?

HE: I don't know.
        [Pause.]
Give me your hand—I want to see what it says.

CONSUELO: A palm reading? Do you know how?

HE: Of course.

CONSUELO: You're a man of many talents, HE.
        [HE studies her hand.]
Will I be rich?

HE: No.

CONSUELO: No?
        [Laughs.]
I'm not sure I like your palm reading!

HE: Shhh!

CONSUELO: What's wrong?

HE: The stars are talking.

CONSUELO: Oh. You're taking this very seriously.

HE: It's a serious matter. When the stars talk, you must listen. Their voices are distant and terrible.
[HE studies her hand.]
You stand at the door of Eternity, Consuelo.

CONSUELO: What does that mean? Will I live a long time?

HE: Yes. This line—see how far it goes? You will live forever.

CONSUELO: *Forever?*

HE: For all eternity!

CONSUELO: *[Smiles.]* Now I think you're only telling me what I want to hear.

HE: No, it's written here. And here. See. You have eternal life, love, and glory—but listen closely … you must not belong to anyone born of earth. If you marry the Baron, Consuelo, you'll die.

CONSUELO: *[Laughs.]* Will he eat me?

HE: Don't laugh at the stars, Consuelo. They're far away, their rays are pale, we can barely see their sleeping shadows, but their sorcery is stern and dark. You stand at the gates of eternity. Your die is cast. You are doomed. And Bezano, who you love in your heart even though you don't know it, he can't save you. He's doomed too. He, too, is a stranger on this earth, submerged in a deep sleep—a little god who has lost himself. Forget Bezano—

CONSUELO: You're scaring me, HE. Why are you saying this?

HE: I'm trying to save you! I'm the only one who can!

CONSUELO: *[Laughs.]* You?

HE: Yes! Don't laugh! Look. Here is the letter H. And the E. HE.

CONSUELO: He Who Gets Slapped? Is the whole thing written there on my palm?

HE: Yes! The stars know everything! Like the strings of a divine harp, spreading their golden rays! Like the hand of God, giving harmony, light, and love to the world! Forget the boy! I love you, Consuelo!

CONSUELO: Let go of my hand.

HE: I speak the language of your awakening! Accept your god, who was thrown down from the summit like a stone! Accept your god who fell to the earth in order to live with you in the drunkenness of joy! Of ecstasy! I love you! I—
> *[CONSUELO slaps HE hard across the face. He steps back.]*

What was that?

CONSUELO: A slap! You forget who you are. You are He Who Gets Slapped! Some god!
> *[Pause.]*

HE: Slap me again.

CONSUELO: What?

HE: I need it for my play. Slap!

CONSUELO: For your play?

HE: Yes.

CONSUELO: Then ... you were only playing? HE ... I'm so sorry. Why did you play so seriously that I believed you? Here, then.
> *[She touches his cheek with her fingertips.]*

HE: You are a queen, and I am the fool who is in love with you. Didn't you know, Consuelo, that every queen has a fool, and he is always in love with her, and they always beat him for it. He Who Gets Slapped.

CONSUELO: No. I didn't know.

HE: Yes. Every queen. Beauty has her fool. Oh, how many fools she has! Her court is crowded with them, and the sound of slaps never ends, even through the night! But I never received such a sweet slap as the one given just now by my little queen.

[The USHER enters, followed by a GENTLEMAN from the audience, dressed in black, very respectable. The USHER points at HE.]

USHER #2: *[To the GENTLEMAN.]* Is he the one?

GENTLEMAN: Yes, thank you.

CONSUELO: *[To HE.]* You have a visitor?

HE: Apparently.

CONSUELO: I'll leave you alone, then. Thank you for cheering me up.
  *[HE nods. CONSUELO exits along with the USHER.
  Silence as the two men stare at one another.]*

GENTLEMAN: Is it really you under all that makeup?

HE: There's no use pretending. You've already figured it out.

GENTLEMAN: I almost don't believe my eyes.

HE: What do you want?

GENTLEMAN: You haven't forgiven me, I see.

HE: Is she here? My wife?

GENTLEMAN: Oh, no! No. I'm all alone.

HE: Have you left her already?

GENTLEMAN: No.
  [Pause.]
We have a son.
  [Pause.]
After your disappearance … when you left that insulting letter—

HE: Insulting? Are you still able to feel insults?
  [Losing his patience.]
Why are you here?! What do you want?!

GENTLEMAN: There are things we need to talk over—

HE: Talk over?! Do you really believe we have anything to talk about?!

GENTLEMAN: Perhaps we should go somewhere a little more discreet. Your home?

HE: This is my home.

GENTLEMAN: Someone might interrupt us.

HE: Talk fast.

GENTLEMAN: May I sit down?

HE: No.
                    [Pause.]

GENTLEMAN: I've been looking for you for almost a year. But tonight … it was a complete accident. I was in town for business. I have no friends here, so I went to the circus of all places. And here you are!
                    [Pause.]
Everybody thinks you're dead. I'm the only one who didn't believe it. I knew somehow. It just didn't seem possible—

HE: Your son—does he look like me?

GENTLEMAN: Why would he look like you?

HE: Widows often have children by the new husband who resemble the old one. Or did you manage to avoid that misfortune?

GENTLEMAN: He's the spitting image of his father.

HE: And your book is a big success, I hear.

GENTLEMAN: Are you trying to insult me?

HE: *[Laughs.]* Touchy, touchy! Why were you trying to find me?

GENTLEMAN: My conscience—

HE: You don't have a conscience.
                    [Pause.]
You want to know what I think? I think you were afraid you hadn't robbed
me of *everything*, so you came back for one more pass—just to make sure.

GENTLEMAN: That's ridiculous.

HE: Would you like my fool's cap with its bells?! Or is it too big for your
bald head?!

GENTLEMAN: It isn't my fault if your wife—

HE: The devil take my wife!
                    [Silence.]

GENTLEMAN: I know you're angry. It's understandable, of course. And
I'm sure my success hasn't helped matters.
                    [HE laughs.]
It wasn't entirely deserved. I admit that.

HE: Not entirely!

GENTLEMAN: But you were always so indifferent to fame and glory.
What does it really matter if a rival finally came along who—

HE: *[Another burst of laughter.]* Rival! You—a rival!

GENTLEMAN: *[Growing pale.]* But my book—

HE: You dare call it that?! *Your* book?! In front of *me?!*
                    [Pause.]

GENTLEMAN: I'm a very unhappy man.

HE: You're a fake—that's what you are. An impostor. You talk about your
book—your great success. And it's true, there isn't a newspaper or journal
to be found in which *you* and *your* book aren't favorably mentioned.
Everyone loves you. You're the man of the hour! Who remembers *me?* No
one. I've been banished to obscurity. And the critics were glad to see me
go, too. It was too much effort to extract thought from my heavy
abstractions. It overworked their poor little brains. But you—the great
vulgarizer! You made my thoughts comprehensible even to pigs and horses!
They don't have to think anymore. They don't have to reason. You've

absolved them of that. They simply read your words and spout them back like some sort of silly mantra. You dressed my Apollo in a second-hand suit, my Venus in a cheap dress, and gave my principled hero the ears of an ass! But what do you care—your career is made. No one is conscious of the theft. They applaud you wherever you go. Other writers imitate you. You'll be known as the father of an important movement. Meanwhile, I can't pick up the paper without being confronted by faces in which I recognize the traits of my own children. My literary children. The fruit of long years of devotion to my craft. Countless hours, locked away in my study, struggling to unlock the secrets of a new language, a new vernacular, stripping away conventions. And I succeeded. I finally did it! Yet, none of my children recognize me. I'm a stranger. They know only you. It isn't enough that you've stolen my wife—you've stolen my children as well! My legacy! And now you come to me because ... why? You feel *guilty?* You want my *blessing?* You want me to pat you on the back and tell you it's okay?! Fine. It's yours. It's all yours. Take it! My wife! My children! My ideas! Assume all rights! You are my lawful heir!

> *[Pause.]*

It's funny. There was a time when I loved you ... even thought you a little gifted. You—my empty shadow.

> *[Pause.]*

GENTLEMAN: I am your shadow. And I hate you for it.

HE: What a comedy!

GENTLEMAN: I'm respected. Famous. I have your wife, yes ... but she still loves *you.* Our favorite discussion is about your genius. She's aware of it, you see. *We* are aware of it. My son—she'll raise him to be like you. She'll mold him into your image. She'll feed him your thoughts. Even in bed, when I hold her in my arms, when I look into her eyes, we're never alone—you are always there, hovering over us like a ghost. And if I try to bury myself in my work, in my books—there you are again! Everywhere! It's always you! I'm never alone! Never myself! Even in my dreams, I find myself staring at your hateful image, looming, as if in some carnival mirror!

HE: It's beautiful—isn't it? The way things turn out. The victim proves to be the thief, and the thief complains of theft!

> *[Laughs.]*

Listen, I was wrong. You aren't my shadow. You're only the crowd. The audience.

GENTLEMAN: I wish you really had died.

HE: Maybe I did.
        [Silence.]
You have nothing to fear from me. I'm never going back. That's why you're here—yes? To make sure?

GENTLEMAN: I … I suppose so. Yes.

HE: Then you have your answer.
        [Pause.]

GENTLEMAN: You won't change your mind?

HE: No. Your secret is safe.
        [Pause.]

GENTLEMAN: All right.
        [Pause.]
Do you mind if … if I visit the circus every now and then? Just to watch you—from the crowd. I won't bother you. I'll keep my distance. I only want to understand your transformation. Knowing you as I do, I can't believe you're here without some sort of *idea*—some plan. But what plan? That is what intrigues me.

HE: The circus turns no one away.

GENTLEMAN: All right, then. Thank you.
        [The GENTLEMAN offers his hand, but HE does not take it.]
You won't take my hand? We're parting forever.

HE: Not forever. We'll meet again in the next life—in the Kingdom of Heaven. I trust you'll be there as well?

GENTLEMAN: *[Hesitates.]* I hope so.
        [The GENTLEMAN goes, leaving HE alone.]

* * *

ACT III

[HE sits alone, motionless. Enter PAULIE and WALLY, playing their kazoos.]

PAULIE: Ah! Morning, HE.

WALLY: We were just rehearsing. For the benefit.

PAULIE: Wally has about as much rhythm as an elephant.

WALLY: I resemble that remark!

HE: Are you preparing something special?

PAULIE: No. The usual.

WALLY: If we'd had more time. But it all happened so fast. You do know it's her last night?

PAULIE: Of course he knows it's her last night. Would she be getting a benefit otherwise?

WALLY: What about you, HE—preparing something special?

HE: Yes.

WALLY: What is it?

HE: You'll have to wait and see.

MANCINI: *[Entering.]* There! A true showman! He doesn't give away all his secrets beforehand!

WALLY: *[With a look at MANCINI.]* Come on, Paulie. Let's rehearse.

PAULIE: Remember—don't dance like an elephant this time. You're an ant!
[WALLY and PAULIE go off, playing.]

MANCINI: I can hardly believe it, HE! We're finally escaping this second-rate circus! And a benefit performance to boot! No more Papa Briquet! No more stupid posters or silly clowns! No offense.

HE: None taken.

MANCINI: Things are finally taking a turn for the better.

HE: How does Consuelo feel about it?

MANCINI: How should she feel? She'll be the wife of an important man. She'll attend receptions, have butlers—

HE: And the girl?

MANCINI: What girl?
                    [Off HE'S look.]
Oh—that. It's taken care of. For a small sum, her parents have agreed to drop all charges. The Baron will pay them off after the ceremony.

HE: Then you've managed to wriggle out of your little predicament.

MANCINI: One of the many benefits of wealth—you can get away with anything.
                    [MANCINI laughs. Enter PAPA BRIQUET.]
Ah! Papa Briquet! I wanted to thank you for this evening's benefit.

PAPA BRIQUET: Don't thank me. It was Xena's idea. If it were up to me, you'd get nothing.

MANCINI: I'm sure your exaggerating.

PAPA BRIQUET: I love Consuelo like a daughter, Mancini. Here she has an honest job, wonderful comrades—what more could she ask for?

MANCINI: I asked you to increase her salary, Briquet. If you'd been more reasonable—

PAPA BRIQUET: Shut up.
                    [Enter CONSUELO in tears.]

CONSUELO: Daddy!

MANCINI: Consuelo?

HE: What's wrong?

CONSUELO: I can't, Daddy! Tell him! He has no right to yell at me!

MANCINI: Who?

CONSUELO: Bezano! He threatened to hit me with his whip!

PAPA BRIQUET: What?!

CONSUELO: I can't work under these conditions!

MANCINI: What kind of operation are you running here, Briquet!

PAPA BRIQUET: Where is he?

CONSUELO: With the horses.

PAPA BRIQUET: I'll talk to him! Threaten to hit you, will he?!
                    [Exit PAPA BRIQUET.]

HE: Did he really threaten you?

CONSUELO: Yes.

HE: He's only jealous, you know.

MANCINI: That's no excuse.

HE: He doesn't want you to go.

CONSUELO: Well, he should have said something before now! It's a little late!

MANCINI: Are you all right, child? You seem different today.

CONSUELO: It's nothing. I'm just … I'm going to miss this place. Everyone. Even Bezano. You should have heard the things he said.

MANCINI: You'll get over it, believe me.

CONSUELO: The Baron promised to make a ring for me to gallop in and buy me the finest horse. Do you think he really means it?

MANCINI: Of course. Barons do not lie.

CONSUELO: I think it will be nice to have money. You can do what you want then.

MANCINI: Exactly!

CONSUELO: But he scares me sometimes. The way he looks at me. Like a spider. Like I'm his fly. You should hear the way he talks. Bezano never talks like that.

MANCINI: Bezano! Bezano is a child—he doesn't dare talk to you like that! The Baron is a real man! You must learn to accept it!

CONSUELO: Why?

MANCINI: All men are like that, child.

CONSUELO: I don't like your advice. You think everyone is as dirty as you.

MANCINI: They are.

HE: Not HE.

MANCINI: Pfff!

CONSUELO: You love me—don't you, HE?

HE: I do, my Queen. I am your fool.

CONSUELO: And when I leave, will you find another queen?

HE: No, I will follow you. I will carry the train of your dress and wipe away your tears.

MANCINI: Idiot!
                    [Laughs.]
You don't know how sorry I am, HE, that I don't live in the days of my ancestors when we had scores of motley fools to kick and slap around. Now, Mancini is compelled to go to this dirty circus to find a good fool— and then, whose fool is he? Mine? No. He belongs to everyone who pays a few dollars.

HE: We are the servants of those who pay.

MANCINI: A sorry state of affairs. Imagine, HE—we are in my castle, I near the fireplace with my glass of wine, you chattering nonsense at my feet, jingling your little bells, diverting me. Then, after a while, I get sick of you and want another fool, so I give you a good kick ... Ah, HE, how wonderful it would be!

HE: It would be marvelous, Mancini! And when the Count tires of my chattering, I will lie down at the feet of my queen!

MANCINI: Of course, I'd throw you a gold coin every now and then to keep you happy. Well, when I become rich, I'll hire you. It's settled.
        [Checks his watch.]
Good lord! It's getting late! I still need to meet with the Baron—we have a few details still to discuss.
        [Exit MANCINI.]

CONSUELO: HE, come and lie down at my feet and tell me something cheerful. I'm in a mood.

HE: Are you going to marry the Baron?

CONSUELO: It looks that way.

HE: Do you remember my prediction?

CONSUELO: What prediction?

HE: That if you marry the Baron ...

CONSUELO: Oh—that. But you were just making fun.

HE: Sometimes one makes fun, and it turns out to be true.

CONSUELO: *[Laughs.]* Well, I guess I'll have to take my chances.

HE: And if you die?

CONSUELO: What is death, really?

HE: Nobody knows. Like love! Nobody knows. But your little hands will grow cold, and your little eyes will close … the music will play without you, and without you Bezano will gallop around the ring, Paulie and Wally will play their kazoos, and Madame Xena will try to make the red lion love her …

CONSUELO: I'm so sad.

HE: Are you crying?

CONSUELO: A little. Why did Bezano yell at me? Is it my fault if I couldn't do anything today?

HE: He loves you, as I love you—only he doesn't know it yet.

CONSUELO: There's something here.
                    [She presses a hand against her heart.]
I must be sick. It hurts.

HE: It's not sickness. It's the charm of the stars, Consuelo. It's the voice of your fate.

CONSUELO: Don't talk nonsense. Not today. The stars don't care about me. I'm so small.

HE: You're bigger than you imagine.

CONSUELO: No. I'm nothing.
                    [Pause.]
Tell me another story—about the blue sea and those gods, you know … who are so beautiful.

HE: Don't go to the Baron.

CONSUELO: Why not?

HE: I don't want you to. I won't allow it.

CONSUELO: Who should I marry then—*you?*
                    [She laughs.]
Are you crazy? "I won't allow it." HE! HE will not allow me! What business is it of yours?

HE: I only want you to be happy.
> *[Pause.]*

CONSUELO: I was happy once. I don't remember any details of my childhood—only a feeling ... there was the sea ... and something ... strange faces ...
> *[She closes her eyes.]*

HE: Remember, Consuelo.

CONSUELO: No.
> *[Opening her eyes.]*

It's gone. Everything. I have no early memories of my father. Isn't that strange? Not one. Only a feeling.
> *[BEZANO appears, confused.]*

Bezano! What do you want?

BEZANO: I ... I came to apologize.

CONSUELO: For what?

BEZANO: The way I acted. Before.

CONSUELO: Are you really sorry—or are you only apologizing because they made you?

BEZANO: I don't know why I got so angry. I'm confused. It's your last performance. I ... I wanted it to be perfect.
> *[Pause.]*

Do you forgive me?

CONSUELO: *[Smiles.]* Of course. Silly boy!

HE: Look at the two of you! Wait—stand there a moment! Yes! Just like that!

CONSUELO: Like Adam and Eve?
> *[She laughs.]*

BEZANO: We should get back to work.

CONSUELO: Let me change my shoes.
> *[She exits. Silence.]*

HE: Do you love her, Bezano?

BEZANO: What?

HE: Do you love her? Our little Consuelo.
> *[Pause.]*

BEZANO: It's none of your business. I don't know you. You came off the street. Why should I trust you?

HE: You don't know me, but you know the Baron well enough. Listen. It's hard for me to say this—she loves you. Save her from the spider. Or don't you see the web he is weaving? Get out of this vicious circle. Take her away! Steal her! Whatever it takes! Kill her if you have to—take her to heaven or the devil! But don't give her to this man!

BEZANO: Kill her?

HE: Or him! Kill the Baron!

BEZANO: And who will kill those who come after him?

HE: She loves you.

BEZANO: Did she tell you that herself?

HE: What a stupid little god you are! But you *are* a god! Why can't you see it? Go to her! You belong together!

BEZANO: You really are a fool! Present your own face for slaps if you like, but leave mine out of it.

HE: Bezano!

BEZANO: I don't want to hear any more of this! I'm not a god. I'm an acrobat.
> *[BEZANO goes out angrily. HE is alone. With a tortured expression, he throws his head back and begins to laugh—soundlessly at first, then louder. After a moment MANCINI enters with the BARON.]*

MANCINI: HE! What a cheerful fellow! Laughing even when he's alone! How many slaps will you get today, HE? Will they ring you like a gong? A funny profession—isn't it, Baron?

BARON: Very strange. Where is the Countess?

MANCINI: I'll find her. You wait here. HE, would you be so kind as to entertain our guest? You won't be bored in his company, Baron—I guarantee it!
>   *[MANCINI exits. Pause.]*

BARON: Don't bother trying to entertain me. I don't like clowns.

HE: I don't like Barons.
>   *[HE puts on his derby hat, takes a chair and, with an*
>   *exaggerated gesture, puts it down heavily in front of the*
>   *BARON. HE sits, imitating the pose of the BARON,*
>   *staring him in the eyes. Silence.]*
Can you be silent very long?

BARON: Very long.

HE: And can you wait very long?

BARON: Very long.

HE: Until you get what you came for?

BARON: Until I get it. And you?

HE: I too.
>   *[They stare at each other silently, their heads close*
>   *together. From the ring one hears the strains of the*
>   *Tango.]*

* * *

ACT IV

[Music in the ring. More disorder backstage than usual. All kinds of costumes are scattered about, hanging on pegs, etc... A huge bouquet of fiery-red roses sits on a table. Three USHERS stand near the door, smoking.]

USHER #1: Ten thousand dollars?!

USHER #2: I'm telling you.

USHER #1: For roses?!

USHER #2: That's right.

USHER #3: I don't believe it.

USHER #2: There's a whole truck-load outside. Stick your head out there—you can smell them a mile away.

USHER #3: Crazy Baron.

USHER #1: What good are that many roses?!

USHER #2: He wants to cover the ring with them—the whole ring.

USHER #1: The whole thing?!

USHER #2: Thousands of roses. Like a carpet. That's what he told them—make it like a carpet.

USHER #1: What a waste!

USHER #3: If I had that kind of money, I wouldn't waste it on roses, I'll tell you that much!

[As XENA enters with HE, all three USHERS suddenly throw away their cigarettes like school boys caught in the act. XENA stares at them.]

XENA: What are you doing here, gentlemen? Your place is at the entrance.

USHER #2: We … we were just taking a quick break.

XENA: Don't leave your places again.

USHER #2: Yes, Ma'am.
                    [The USHERS exit quickly. XENA notices the roses.]

XENA: More roses. They're everywhere.

HE: Are you jealous, Madame Xena?

XENA: You're malicious tonight, HE. Don't you approve of Consuelo's marriage?

HE: It's an honest marriage. Even spiders need to improve their stock. Can you imagine what charming spiders this couple will create—with the head of their mother, Consuelo, and the stomach of their father, the Baron! A suitable ornament for any circus ring!

XENA: Why are you out of makeup?

HE: I'm in the third act. I have time.
                    [Pause.]
Do you approve—of the marriage?

XENA: If you ask me, Consuelo sold herself too cheap. What is the Baron worth—a few million? She could have done much better.

HE: She's doing it for her father.

XENA: The Count, you mean?
                    [Laughs.]
You haven't guessed yet? Mancini isn't her father.

HE: What! Does she know?

XENA: No. Why should she know? He found her on the street. Adopted her, of course—legally, she's his daughter. But he wanted her for business purposes. She's been supporting him for years.

HE: It's curious, isn't it—there's more blue blood in her little finger than in all of Mancini. One would think she found *him* on the street and not the other way around!

XENA: Let her go, HE. She's already made up her mind.

HE: Diamonds and butlers?

XENA: When did you ever see a beauty like her content to struggle along with the rest of us? If this one doesn't buy her, another one will. The rich buy up everything beautiful and lock it away, out of sight, in their mansions. It's the way of the world, HE. For the first few years, she'll be a sad beauty, loyal to her husband, but sick inside. Later, she'll begin to attract the eyes of strangers on the sidewalk—and finally, she will take—

HE: Her chauffeur or butler as a lover?

XENA: Not a bad guess. You can't fight Fate. Don't be offended, my friend. I like you. But you aren't beautiful, or young, or rich—what does it matter what you "want" or "don't want"? There is only one way for you. To forget.
> *[Enter PAPA BRIQUET and MANCINI who wears a new suit.]*

MANCINI: Madame Xena! You are dazzling, tonight! Your lion would be a fool if he did not kiss your hand as I do!
> *[He kisses her hand.]*

XENA: Congratulations, Count.

MANCINI: Yes, *merci*.

PAPA BRIQUET: Xena, the Count wants to pay immediately for the breach of contract with Consuelo. Do you remember how much it is?

XENA: Three thousand.

MANCINI: Is that all? For Consuelo? I'll tell the Baron.

XENA: You took—

PAPA BRIQUET: *[To XENA.]* Don't—

XENA: Count, you drew in advance, I wrote it down, one hundred dollars. Will you pay that too?

MANCINI: Of course. Three thousand one hundred.
            [Laughs.]
I never knew I could be so accurate.
            [Seriously.]
Listen, Consuelo and the Baron expressed a desire to bid the whole cast farewell.

HE: The Baron, too?

MANCINI: Yes. They want to do it at intermission. So if you could gather everyone—

PAPA BRIQUET: Of course.

MANCINI: And HE, if you could run to the buffet and ask about the champagne, bottles and glasses—that sort of thing?

HE: Your wish is my command.

MANCINI: Wait a minute—is that a new costume? You look like a devil in that outfit!

HE: Not a devil, Count—just a poor sinner who the devils are frying a little.
            [HE exits, bowing like a clown.]

MANCINI: That fellow is gifted, but too cunning for his own good.

PAPA BRIQUET: It's the Tango color—in honor of your daughter. He needs it for a new stunt he's doing. Some kind of surprise.

MANCINI: *[Sits and looks about the room.]* You know … I'm actually sorry to leave you, old friend. I know it's hard to believe, destined as I am for high society, castles, the company of noblemen … but where else could I find such freedom and … simplicity.
            [Pause.]
By the way—how do you like my new suit?

XENA: I like it. You look like a nobleman of the courts of long ago.

MANCINI: You don't think it's too conspicuous—do you? I mean, who wears lace and satin nowadays? Is this jabot out of place?

XENA: No. It's perfect.

[HE returns, carrying a basket of champagne and glasses.]

MANCINI: Ah! Thank you, HE.
[Checking his watch.]
Good lord! The act's about to end! I have to go!
[MANCINI hurries out.]

PAPA BRIQUET: The devil take him!

XENA: Not so loud!

PAPA BRIQUET: High society! Castles! Noblemen! He's a common swindler!
[Enter JACKSON.]

JACKSON: What an audience! No laughter! Nothing! They've forgotten how!

PAPA BRIQUET: A benefit performance crowd.

JACKSON: In the orchestra, I saw some Barons and a few Egyptian mummies, I think. They just stare at you as if you'd stolen their wallet. You'll have to take a good many slaps tonight, HE, if you want any reaction out of *them.*

HE: Don't worry, Jackson. I'll avenge you.

XENA: How is Bezano?

JACKSON: Bezano! A madman! He's going to break his neck tonight!

PAPA BRIQUET: *[To XENA.]* You must have inspired him.

XENA: What's eating you?

PAPA BRIQUET: Nothing. I don't like all these Barons in my circus. It makes me feel like a swindler instead of an honest artist.

JACKSON: There's something to that.

PAPA BRIQUET: Let's be honest—the foxes have come to steal our hen.

[Enter PAULIE and WALLY, along with several other performers.]

WALLY: Is it time for champagne yet?

PAPA BRIQUET: No!

WALLY: All right, all right.

PAULIE: HE, did you see how the Count walks in his new suit?
[PAULIE imitates MANCINI. Laughter.]

JACKSON: *[Peeking onstage.]* It's almost intermission. Consuelo is galloping now. It's her waltz. They love her!

WALLY: She's so beautiful!
[Suddenly, a crash as if a broken wall were tumbling down: applause, shouting, screaming. The performers begin pouring champagne. More performers enter, in costume, talking and laughing.]
They're coming!

JACKSON: What a success!

PAPA BRIQUET: Silence! Silence, please! Here they come!
[Enter CONSUELO, on the arm of the BARON who is stiff and erect. In his button-hole, the BARON wears a fiery-red rose. MANCINI follows, serious and happy. Behind them, more performers enter, crying: "Bravo, bravo!"]

CONSUELO: Friends … oh, I'm so … Father, I can't—
[She throws herself into MANCINI'S arms and hides her face on his shoulder. MANCINI looks with a reassuring smile over her head at the BARON. The BARON smiles slightly, but remains stiff and motionless. A new burst of applause.]

PAPA BRIQUET: Enough! Enough!

MANCINI: Calm yourself, child. See how they all love you!
> [CONSUELO looks around at everyone. She laughs
> and cries at the same time.]

Ladies and gentlemen, yesterday Baron Regnard did me the honor to ask for my daughter's hand in marriage—
> [Applause.]

—the Countess Veronica, whom you know simply as "Consuelo." Please take your glasses.

CONSUELO: No, tonight I am still Consuelo! I shall always be Consuelo! Oh, Xena!
> [She falls on XENA'S neck. Fresh applause.]

PAPA BRIQUET: Stop it! Silence! Take your glasses! What are you standing there for? If you came, then take your glasses!
> [The performers take their glasses. CONSUELO stands
> near the BARON. In her hand, she holds a glass of
> champagne, which spills over.]

BARON: Be careful, Consuelo. You're going to spill.

CONSUELO: I'm sorry! I'm so nervous! Aren't you, Father?

MANCINI: Silly child.

PAPA BRIQUET: [Stepping forward and raising his glass.] Countess! As the manager of this circus, who was happy enough … to witness … many times … your success—

CONSUELO: Stop it! I am Consuelo! What do you want to do—make me cry? Stop with this "Countess" nonsense. Give me a kiss, Briquet!
> [PAPA BRIQUET kisses her with tears. Laughter,
> applause. The clowns cluck like hens. The other
> performers become more and more lively. In the midst
> of them, the BARON stands motionless. There is a wide
> space around him. Others clink glasses with him and
> quickly move away. With CONSUELO, they clink
> willingly and cheerfully. She kisses them all. BEZANO
> appears in the crowd.]

JACKSON: *[Raising his glass.]* Consuelo, as of today, I extinguish my sun. Let the dark night come after you leave us. It was a pleasure to work with you. We all love you and will treasure the traces of your little feet on the sand. Nothing else remains to us.

CONSUELO: *[Kissing him.]* Oh, Jackson! You are so good! There is no one better!

WALLY: What about me?

CONSUELO: *[Laughs.]* Except for you, Wally!
                *[More laughter. CONSUELO notices BEZANO in the
                crowd.]*
Bezano! Come! I was looking for you!

BEZANO: *[Keeping his distance.]* My congratulations, Countess.

CONSUELO: Don't be silly! I am always your Consuelo!

BEZANO: In the ring, yes. But here ... I congratulate you, Countess.
                *[He steps forward and clinks her glass—then moves
                away. CONSUELO stares after him. MANCINI looks
                at the BARON with a smile. The BARON stands
                motionless.]*

PAPA BRIQUET: Bezano, what's wrong with you? Don't be an ass!

CONSUELO: No, it's all right.
                [Silence.]

PAPA BRIQUET: Enough, enough! Intermission is over! Get back to work!

WALLY: Already?

CONSUELO: Not yet! Please? Just a few more minutes!

PAPA BRIQUET: All right. It's fine. They can wait.
                [From the ring, a Tango can be heard. Exclamations.]

CONSUELO: My Tango! Oh, I want to dance! Who will dance with me?
                [She looks around, towards BEZANO who turns away.]
Who then?

MANCINI: The Baron! Let the Baron dance!

OTHERS: Yes! The Baron!

BARON: All right.
> *[He takes CONSUELO'S arm.]*

I don't know the Tango, but I shall hold tight.
> *[He stands heavily and awkwardly, still holding
> CONSUELO'S arm—an expression of the utmost
> seriousness on his face.]*

MANCINI: *[Applauding.]* Bravo! Bravo!
> *[CONSUELO makes a few restless movements—then
> pulls away.]*

CONSUELO: No, I can't! This is stupid! Let me go!
> *[She runs to XENA and buries her face on the older
> woman's shoulder. The music continues to play. The
> BARON moves quietly to the side. There is an
> uncomfortable silence among the performers.]*

MANCINI: *[Alone.]* Bravo! Bravo! It's charming! Exquisite!

PAPA BRIQUET: Shut up, Mancini.
> *[Silence.]*

HE: *[Holding up his glass.]* Baron, will you permit me to make a toast?

BARON: Make it.

HE: To your dance!
> *[Slight laughter from the performers.]*

BARON: I don't dance!

HE: In that case, let us drink to those who know how to wait longer, until they get it.

BARON: I don't accept toasts I can't understand. Speak plainly.

JACKSON: That's enough, HE. The Baron doesn't like jokes.

HE: But I only want to drink with him.

[As the Tango ends, a buzzer sounds.]

PAPA BRIQUET: *[Relieved.]* There! To the ring, ladies and gentlemen!
To the ring!

> *[As the performers make their way back to the ring,
> MANCINI rushes to the BARON and whispers excitedly
> into his ear. HE approaches CONSUELO, who sits
> alone.]*

CONSUELO: Don't make him angry, HE. Did you see how he pressed my
arm? I wanted to scream.

> *[With tears in her eyes.]*

He hurt me.

HE: It's not too late, Consuelo. Refuse him.

CONSUELO: No. It *is* too late.

HE: Do you want to marry him?

CONSUELO: Don't talk about it. He's watching us.

HE: I'll take you away from here.

CONSUELO: Where?

> *[Laughs.]*

How pale you are! Do you love me too? Don't, HE. Why do they all love
me—all the wrong ones?

HE: You are so beautiful!

CONSUELO: I was okay. I had made up my mind. But when everyone
started speaking so nicely … when they said their goodbyes as if I were
dying, I thought I would die for real. Don't talk. Don't talk. Drink … to
my happiness.

> *[With a sad smile.]*

To my happiness, HE. What are you doing?

HE: I'm throwing away the glass you drank from with the others. I'll get
you another. Wait a minute.

> *[HE goes to the table and pours another glass of
> champagne. MANCINI approaches CONSUELO.]*

MANCINI: Come. The Baron is waiting.

CONSUELO: Not yet.

MANCINI: It's indecent. The Baron is waiting, and you talk here with this clown. Everyone is watching. They're looking at you.

CONSUELO: *[Loudly.]* Leave me alone, Father! HE is my friend! I will come when I'm ready!

BARON: Don't, Count. Let her be.
            [To CONSUELO.]
Talk to whomever you please for as long as you like. There's no hurry.
            *[HE returns with champagne. The BARON and
            MANCINI give them room.]*

HE: Here is your glass. To your happiness. To your freedom, Consuelo.

CONSUELO: Where is yours? You won't drink with me?

HE: Leave half.

CONSUELO: All right.
            [She drinks.]
I'm going to be drunk.

HE: No. You won't be drunk. You forget, I'm a magician. I charmed the wine. My witchery is in it. Drink, goddess.

CONSUELO: What kind eyes you have. But why are you so pale?

HE: Because I love you. Look at my kind eyes and drink. Give yourself up to my charms, Consuelo. Sleep. And when you awake, you will see your sky, your ocean, your gods …

CONSUELO: *[Drinking.]* I'll see all that? Really?

HE: Yes! You will emerge from the sky blue waters … the whisper of foam at your marble feet …

CONSUELO: There. Exactly half.
            [She gives the half-full glass to HE.]
What's wrong with you? Are you laughing or crying?

HE: I am laughing. And crying.

MANCINI: *[Pushing HE aside.]* Enough. My patience is exhausted. The Baron has been good enough to allow it, but I am your father, and I have had enough. Your arm, Countess! Step aside, sir.

CONSUELO: I'm tired.

MANCINI: You're not too tired to chatter and drink wine with a clown. Briquet! Ring the bell—it's time.

CONSUELO: I need to sit down.

MANCINI: Come along.

XENA: Don't be cruel, Mancini. Look how pale she is.

BARON: What's wrong?

CONSUELO: Nothing.

XENA: Let her sit. She needs to rest.

MANCINI: Nonsense! She can rest after!

CONSUELO: Are the roses ready?

XENA: Yes, dear. The roses are ready. You'll have such an extraordinary carpet. No one will ever forget.
                    [Suddenly CONSUELO cries out in pain.]

BARON: What's wrong?

XENA: What is it?

PAPA BRIQUET: Consuelo?

CONSUELO: It hurts!

XENA: What hurts?

MANCINI: Are you sick?

XENA: It's all the excitement.

CONSUELO: It hurts! Here!
>   *[She holds her heart.]*

MANCINI: Bring a doctor!

CONSUELO: What is it, Father? I'm afraid! My feet ... I ... I can't stand
…
>   *[CONSUELO collapses. MANCINI carries her to a*
>   *couch.]*

PAPA BRIQUET: What's going on?

BARON: You heard him! A doctor!

HE: It's no use.

BARON: What?

HE: She's dying.

BARON: Dying! Don't be—

HE: You waited too long, Baron. You should have snatched her away when
you had the chance.

BARON: What are you saying?

HE: I killed her.

BARON: You—what?!

MANCINI: You're lying! Damned clown! What did you give her? Did
you poison her? Bring a doctor!

HE: It's too late. There's nothing you can do.
>   *[To CONSUELO.]*
You're dying, my Queen.

CONSUELO: Are you joking again, HE? Don't frighten me. I'm so frightened. Is this death? I don't want it. HE, tell me you're joking.
            [Pause.]
You ... you said I would live forever.

HE: You will. But sleep first. Sleep.

CONSUELO: Yes ... so tired ...

HE: Can you see the light?

CONSUELO: Yes ... is it the ring? My roses?

HE: No ... it is the sea and the sun ... can you feel the sea foam on your ankles? Can you feel it?

CONSUELO: Yes ...

HE: You are flying to the sun. You have no body. You are flying higher. I am the sea foam. It shines ... so strong ...
            [CONSUELO dies. The others rush to her.]

MANCINI: Is ... is she sleeping?

XENA: *[Holding CONSUELO'S dead hand.]* No.
            [The BARON and HE are motionless, each in his place.]

JACKSON: The only thing left is the trace of her little feet in the sand.
            [To HE.]
It would have been better if you had never come to us.
            [There is music in the ring.]

PAPA BRIQUET: The music! Stop the music! What is happening?!
            [The BARON takes the rose from his button-hole and drops it to the ground.]

XENA: *[To PAPA BRIQUET.]* Call the police.

MANCINI: *[Awakening from his stupor, screams.]* The police! Call the police! It's murder! I am Count Mancini! I am Count Mancini! They will cut off your head! Murderer! Damned clown! Thief! I will kill you myself!

[MANCINI produces the derringer from the handle of his cane and aims it at HE—but before he can fire, the BARON wrestles it from him.]

BARON: No.
[HE collapses with a laugh. A tremor shakes his body.]

JACKSON: It's true, then. He poisoned himself as well.

BARON: I'm going for the police.
[Pause.]
I am a witness. I saw. I saw how he put poison ... I—
[The BARON exits with the derringer. A moment later, a shot is heard in the corridor. JACKSON rushes out.]

JACKSON: *[Returning.]* The Baron ... he ...

MANCINI: The Baron? The Baron?! But ... he ... no!
[HE bursts out laughing.]

PAPA BRIQUET: Stop it! What's wrong with you? A man just killed himself! Why are you laughing?

HE: He really did love her! In spite of everything! He loved her after all! It's the last slap! He wants to be ahead of me even *there!* But I won't let him! I'm coming! I'm coming, my queen! I won't let him have you!
[HE clutches his throat and dies. General agitation.]

* * *

CALL OF THE REVOLUTION

by LEONID ANDREYEV

adapted for the stage by WALTER WYKES

CHARACTERS:

MAN
WOMAN

> *[A modest home—sparsely furnished. Moonlight pours in through an open window, illuminating the otherwise unlit room. A WOMAN stands in front of the window, motionless, staring out into the darkness. A candle flickers in her hands. She is trembling. After a few moments, a MAN appears from the hallway.]*

WOMAN: Did you hear?

MAN: Come to bed.

WOMAN: You didn't?

MAN: Hear what?

WOMAN: Outside. They're building barricades.

MAN: Where?

WOMAN: Here. On our street.
> *[They lock eyes for a long moment—the MAN's face turns pale. He goes to the window. The WOMAN continues to tremble, but her eyes remain locked on the man, motionless, gauging his reaction.]*

MAN: How long?

WOMAN: An hour at least.
> *[Pause.]*

MAN: My brother?

WOMAN: He's gone. He knew you'd try to stop him, so he left as soon as it started. I saw him go.

MAN: Why didn't you wake me?

WOMAN: What could you have done?
> *[Silence.]*

MAN: It's really happening. I can't believe it.
> *[She clasps his hand.]*

WOMAN: Are you afraid?

MAN: Are you?
> *[She shakes her head "no," but cannot control her trembling.]*

I had a feeling it would happen. A premonition. It's been too quiet. There's been nothing for days now. The factories have been closed. The roads have been almost empty. Even the air feels cleaner. I went outside tonight ... there were no lights, no cars, nothing. Not a single sound of the city, just ... quiet. If you closed your eyes you really would have thought you were somewhere far out in the country. It had that smell, you know, whatever it is—that smell of spring nights—of fields and flowers and dew. I heard a dog bark, and it rang out so clear. It struck me ... you never notice things in the city—there's too much going on. It made me laugh.
> *[A dog barks.]*

Listen, a dog is barking now.
> *[Somewhere, hammers begin to pound. The WOMAN rushes to the window and points.]*

WOMAN: There they are again! On the corner!
> *[They stare out into the darkness, holding each other. The blows of an axe join in the clamor.]*

It sounds so cheerful, so resonant, like in a forest or a river when you're mending a boat or building a dam. Cheerful, harmonious work.

MAN: It's the sound of the future.
> *[Silence.]*

I have to go too, you know.

WOMAN: I knew you would.

MAN: You understand then?

WOMAN: Of course.

MAN: It's my duty.

WOMAN: And the children?

MAN: You'll be with them. They'll have a mother—that will have to be enough. I can't stay behind.

WOMAN: And I? Can I?

MAN: What?
>
> *[Surprised, he stretches out his hands, but she pushes them aside.]*

WOMAN: Something like this happens once in what—a hundred years? A thousand? Do you really expect me to stay here and change diapers?

MAN: Do you want to die? They'll kill you just as quickly as they will me. They won't hesitate because you're a woman.

WOMAN: *[Still trembling.]* I'm not afraid.

MAN: And what about the children—without you to look after them, what chance do they have?

WOMAN: This is bigger than the children.

MAN: What if they die?

WOMAN: What if they *do* die? If it's for the cause?

MAN: Are you really saying this—are you speaking these words?! *You* who have lived for nothing but those children?! Who have been filled with fear for them day and night?!

WOMAN: That was before.

MAN: What's come over you?!

WOMAN: The same thing that's come over you. I can see the future.

MAN: You want to go with me?

WOMAN: Yes!
>
> *[Pause.]*

Don't be angry. Please. But tonight … when the sounds began … when the hammers and the axes began to fall … you were still asleep … and I suddenly understood that my husband, my children—all these things are temporary.... I love you very much …
>
> *[She clasps his hand again.]*

... but can't you hear how they are hammering out there?! They are pounding away, and something seems to be falling, breaking apart, some kind of wall seems to be coming down—the earth is changing—and it is so spacious and wide and free! It's night now, but it seems to me the sun is shining! I'm thirty years old and already I'm like an old woman, I know it, you can see it in my face. And yet ... tonight I feel like I'm only seventeen, and that I've fallen in love for the first time—a great, boundless love that lights up the sky!

MAN: It's as if the city were already dead and gone. You're right, I feel like a kid, too.

WOMAN: They're pounding, and it sounds to me like music, like singing of which I've always dreamt—all my life—and I didn't know who it was that I loved with such a boundless love, which made me feel like crying and laughing and singing! This is freedom! Don't deny me my place—let me die with those who are working out there, who are calling in the future so bravely and rousing the dead past from its grave!

MAN: [Strangely.] There is no such thing as time.

WOMAN: What?

MAN: The sun rises and sets ... the hand moves around the dial ... but time doesn't exist. It's an illusion. Who are you? I don't know you. Are you a human being?

> [The WOMAN bursts into ringing laughter, as if she really were only seventeen years old.]

WOMAN: I don't know you, either! Are you a human being, too? How strange ... how beautiful it is—two human beings!

MAN: I have to go. I can't wait any longer.

WOMAN: Wait, I'll give you something to eat. You should eat first. A few more minutes won't make any difference. See how sensible I am. I'll come tomorrow. I'll give the children away and find you.

MAN: Comrade.

WOMAN: Yes, comrade.
> *[The strokes of the axe can be heard through the open window. She gives him some bread to eat—sets it on the table, but he only stares at it.]*

Why don't you eat?

MAN: Bread—it's so strange. Everything is so mysterious and new. I feel like laughing. I look at the walls and they seem so ... temporary. They're almost invisible. I can see how they've been built—how they will be destroyed. Everything will pass. The table ... the food on it ... you and I ... this city ... everything seems so transparent and light.
> *[The WOMAN glances at the stale, dry crust of bread. She turns her head slightly, very slightly, in the direction where the children are sleeping.]*

Do you feel sorry for them? The children? That they've come into the world now? This time of all times?
> *[She shakes her head without removing her eyes from the bread.]*

WOMAN: No ... I was only thinking of our life before.
> *[Pause.]*

How incomprehensible it seems! It's like waking from a long dream.
> *[She surveys the room with her eyes.]*

Is this really the place where we lived?

MAN: You were my wife.

WOMAN: And they were our children.

MAN: We worked.

WOMAN: We made love.

MAN: We paid our bills at this table.

WOMAN: How we sweated over those bills!

MAN: It seems so pointless now—doesn't it? All that worrying over a few dollars here or there.

WOMAN: And here, beyond this wall, your father died.

MAN: Yes. He died in his sleep. He told me this day would come—but he didn't live to see it.

> *[The sound of a baby crying comes suddenly from the hallway.]*

Her cry seems so strange now … amidst these phantom walls, while there, below, they're building barricades.

> *[The WOMAN, jolted out of her dream, moves towards the sound.]*

WOMAN: Well, go!

MAN: Wait. I want to kiss them first.

WOMAN: You'll wake them up.

MAN: You're right.

> *[The WOMAN disappears into the hallway. The MAN goes to the window and stares out into the darkness. The pounding continues. The baby's cry subsides. After a few moments, the WOMAN returns.]*

WOMAN: Will you take your gun?

MAN: Yes.

WOMAN: It's behind the stove.

> *[He retrieves the gun.]*

MAN: Well …

> *[She kisses him.]*

What unfamiliar … what strange eyes! For ten years I've looked into these eyes—I've known them better than my own—and now there's something new in them … something entirely new … something I can't define.

WOMAN: Will you remember me?

MAN: Of course.

WOMAN: How can you be sure? Everything will be different now.

MAN: I'll remember.

WOMAN: And if you die?

MAN: I don't know.

> *[He looks around at the walls, at the bread, at the candle. He takes his wife by the hand and moves towards the door. A pause.]*

Well ... 'till we meet again!

WOMAN: Yes ... 'till we meet again!

> *[He goes out into the darkness. She watches after him as the sounds of hammers and axes fill the air.]*

* * *

THE SERPENT'S TALE

by LEONID ANDREYEV

adapted for the stage by WALTER WYKES

CHARACTERS:

A WOMAN

[A WOMAN sways rhythmically. Her eyes closed, she seems to be aware of nothing but the hypnotic movement of her own body. She is terribly beautiful.]

[After a few moments, her eyes flash open, and a half-smile creeps across her face. She places a finger gently to her lips.]

WOMAN: Shhh! Shhh! Shhh! Come closer. Look into my eyes!

I always was a fascinating creature, you know. Tender, sensitive, thoughtful. I was wise beyond my years. And so flexible in the writhing of my graceful body. It will give you pleasure to watch me dance—will it not? Shall I dance for you? Shall I coil up into a ring? Shall I flash my scales and wind myself around? Shall I clasp you to my steel body in a gentle, cold embrace? One of many! One of many!

Shhh! Shhh! Look into my eyes!

Why do you look away? Don't you like my writhing and my straight, piercing gaze? Oh, my head is heavy—therefore I sway quietly. My head is heavy—therefore I gaze straight ahead as I sway. Come closer. I want to feel your warmth. That's right—stroke my wise forehead with your fingers; in its fine outlines you will find the form of a cup into which flows knowledge, the dew of the evening-flowers. When I stir the air by my writhing, a trace is left in it—the design of the finest of webs, the web of dream-charms, the enchantment of noiseless movements, the inaudible hiss of gliding lines. I am silent and I sway myself. I look ahead and I sway. What is this strange burden I carry on my neck?

I love you.

I always was a fascinating creature, and those that I loved were loved tenderly and truly. Come closer. Come. Do you see my teeth? My white, sharp, enchanting little teeth? I used to bite when I kissed, you know. Not painfully, no—just a nibble. A tender caress. I would bite until the first bright drops of blood appeared, until a cry came forth which sounded like the tinkling of a bell. It was very pleasant—do not think otherwise; if my little bite was unwelcome, those whom I kissed would not have come back for more—would they? And they did come back! They came as if drawn by some irresistible force—by the pull of the moon! They could not help themselves! And I kissed them many times! It is only now that I can kiss but once—how sad—only once! One kiss for each—how little that is for a loving heart, for a sensitive soul, striving for a perfect union! But it is only I, the sad one, who kisses once, and must seek love again—my lover knows no other love after mine: to him my one, tender, nuptial kiss is binding and eternal. I will not deceive you. Be patient, and when my story is ended—I will kiss you too.

I love you.

Look into my eyes. Is it not true that my eyes are magnificent and enchanting? Have you ever seen such a firm look, a straight look? It is steadfast, like steel forced against your heart. I look ahead and sway myself, I look and I enchant; in my green eyes I gather your fear, your loving, fatigued, submissive longing. Come closer. I am a queen now and you cannot fail to see my beauty; but there was a time once—ah, what a strange time! The thought of it troubles me—what a strange and confusing time! No one loved me. No one worshipped me. I was persecuted with such cruelty, trampled in the mud and jeered—Ah, what a strange time it was! One of many! One of many!

I told you to come closer—did I not?

Why did they not love me? Was I not a fascinating creature then, as I am now? Only then I lacked malice; I was gentle and kind-hearted, and I danced wonderfully. But they tortured me. They burnt me with fire. Those heavy, coarse beasts trampled upon me ... their terrible weight pressing down ... cold tusks and bloody mouths tore my tender body—and in my powerless sorrow I bit the sand, I swallowed the dust of the ground—I nearly died of despair. I was near death every day, crushed. Every day I was dying of despair. Oh, what a terrible time it was! Do you not pity me? The stupid forest has forgotten everything—it does not remember that time, but I remember. Come closer. Comfort me—me, the offended, the sad one, the loving one who dances so beautifully.

I love you.

You understand me—do you not? You alone? How was I to defend myself? I had only my white, wonderful, sharp little teeth—they were good only for kisses. How could I defend myself from those terrible beasts? It is only now that I carry on my neck this terrible burden of a head, and my look is commanding and straight, but then my head was light and my eyes gazed meekly. Then I had not yet any poison. Oh, my head is so heavy, it is hard for me to hold it up! I have grown tired of my look—two stones are in my forehead, and these are my eyes. Perhaps the glittering stones are precious—but it is hard to carry them instead of gentle eyes—they oppress my brain. It is so hard for my head! I look ahead and sway myself; I see you in a green mist—you are so far away. Come closer—come and brace me up. You are very strong—are you not? Come and show me your strength. I am trembling.

You see, even in sorrow I am beautiful. I am only weak because of love. Look into my pupil; I will narrow and widen it, and give it a peculiar glitter—the twinkling of a star at night, the playfulness of all precious stones—of diamonds, of green emeralds, of yellowish topaz, of blood-red rubies. Look into my eyes: It is I, the queen—I am crowning myself, and that which is glittering, burning and glowing—that robs you of your reason, your freedom and your life—it is poison. It is a drop of my venom. But I warned you—did I not?

How has this happened? I cannot say. I bear you no ill-will—you nor the others. One of many!

I lived and suffered. I was silent. I languished. I hid myself when I could; I crawled away hastily. But they pursued me without mercy—until I could no longer weep, they pursued me! I, who wept such great tears, such wonderful tears of passion—I cannot weep; and my easy dance grew ever faster and ever more beautiful. Alone in the stillness, alone in the thicket, I danced with sorrow in my heart—they despised my swift dance and would have killed me if they could. Suddenly my head began to grow heavy ... how strange it is! My head grew heavy, just as small and beautiful, just as wise and beautiful, it had suddenly grown terribly heavy; it bent my neck to the ground, and hurt my delicate body. Now I am somewhat used to it, but at first it was dreadfully awkward and painful. I thought I was going to die. But I did not die.

And suddenly ... come closer now ... look into my eyes. Shhh! Shhh! Shhh!

And suddenly my look became heavy—it became fixed and strange—even I was frightened! I was frightened of myself! I wanted to turn and glance away—but I could not. I could only look straight ahead, as I do now—I could only pierce with my eyes ever more deeply; I was petrified—look into my eyes—just as everything I look upon becomes petrified. Look into my eyes.

I love you. Do not laugh at my story. If you do, I shall be cross. I shall not give myself to you. And I want to open my heart, my sensitive heart, I want to share with you everything, my whole being, my essence! I want you to understand my suffering. I want a consort, an equal, a perfect union ... but it is not possible. All my efforts are in vain—I am alone. I will always be alone. My first and final kiss is full of rippling sorrow—and the one I love is not here, and I must seek love again, and tell my tale from the beginning, if only to hear a familiar voice—my heart cannot bare itself, and the poison torments me and my head grows heavier. Am I not beautiful in my despair? Come closer.

I am almost ready to kiss you.

Once I was bathing in the forest—I love to be clean—it is a sign of noble birth, and I bathe frequently. While bathing, dancing in the water, I saw my reflection, and as always, fell in love with myself. I am so fond of beautiful things! And suddenly I saw—on my forehead, among my other inborn adornments, a new sign ... a strange sign ... Perhaps it was this sign that brought the heaviness, the petrified look, and the sweet taste in my mouth. Here a cross is darkly outlined on my forehead—right here—look. Come closer. Is it not strange? I did not understand at the time; I liked it—I thought it beautiful. But on the same day, on that same terrible day, when the cross appeared, my first kiss became also my last—my kiss became fatal.

Even now, I can taste the venom. I am preparing it for you. I was always fond of precious stones, but think, beloved, how much more precious is a little drop of my poison. It is such a little drop. Have you ever seen it? Never, never. But you shall. You shall see! Consider how much suffering, painful humiliation, powerless rage I had to endure in order to bring forth this one little drop. I am a queen! In this tiny drop, I carry death unto the living, and my kingdom is limitless, even as grief is limitless, even as death is limitless. I am a queen! My look is inexorable. My dance is terrible! I am beautiful! One of many! One of many!

Oh! Come closer. Come to me. My story is not yet ended.

That day, I crawled into the cursed forest, into my green dominion. I was a queen, and like a queen I bowed graciously to the right and to the left. And they—they ran away! Like a queen I bowed to my subjects—and they, queer people—they ran. Why did they run? Look into my eyes. Do you see in them anything frightening—a terrible glimmer and a flash? Do you feel fear? Do the rays of my crown blind your eyes? Are you petrified?

Are you lost? I shall soon dance my last dance—do not fall. I shall coil into rings, I shall flash my scales dimly, and I shall clasp my steel body to you in a gentle, cold embrace. Here I am! Accept my only kiss, my nuptial kiss— it is the deadly grief of all oppressed lives. One of many! One of many!

I love you.

Die!

* * *

DATE DUE

MAY 04 2015 ILL# 14546783 PNU

CPSIA information can be obtained at www.ICGtesting.com

226045LV00001B/266/A

9 781430 320555